STORIES OF BEOWULF

TOLD TO THE CHILDREN

By H. E. MARSHALL

Stories of Beowulf: Told to the Children
By H. E. Marshall
Illustrated by J. R. Skelton

Print ISBN 13: 978-1-4209-7351-8
eBook ISBN 13: 978-1-4209-7413-3

Cover Image: a detail of an illustration from the book by J. R. Skelton, first published by E. P. Dutton & co., New York, 1908.

Please visit *www.digireads.com*

CONTENTS

About This Book

'Beowulf is known to every one.' Some months ago I read these words, and doubted if they were true. Then the thought came to me that I would help to make them true, for Beowulf is a fine story finely told, and it is a pity that there should be any who do not know it. So here it is "told to the children."

Besides being a fine story, Beowulf is of great interest because it is our earliest epic, that is, the oldest poem in the Anglo-Saxon language which tells of noble deeds in noble words.

In the British Museum there is a little book, worn and brown with age, spoiled by fire and water. Yet it is not so brown and old, it is not so spoiled but that it may still be read by those who know Anglo-Saxon. This book is a thousand years old, and in its worn brown pages it holds the story of Beowulf.

There is something strange and wonderful in the thought that the story which pleased our forefathers a thousand years ago should please us still to-day. But what is more wonderful is that it should be told in such beautiful words that they thrill us with delight and make us feel as if those old days were fresh and living. In the telling of the story I have tried to keep something of that old-time spirit, and when, later, you come to read the tale in bigger and better books, I hope that you will say that I did not quite fail.

H.E. MARSHALL.

Oxford, 1908.

Chapter I. How Grendel the Ogre Warred with the Dane Folk

Long, long ago, there lived in Daneland a king called Hrothgar. The old men of his country loved him and bowed the knee to him gladly, and the young men obeyed him and joyfully did battle for him. For he was a king mighty in war, and valiant. Never foe could stand against him, but he overcame them all, and took from them much spoil.

So this king wrought peace in his land and his riches grew great. In his palace there were heaped gold in rings and in chains, armour finely welded, rich jewels which glowed as soft sunlight.

Then King Hrothgar looked upon this great treasure and brooded thereon. At last he said, 'I will build me a great hall. It shall be vast and wide, adorned within and without with gold and ivory, with gems and carved work. The fame of it shall spread over all the earth, and men shall sing of it for all time. And when it is builded, therein shall I call all my warriors, young and old and divide to them the treasure that I have. It shall be a hall of joy and feasting.'

Then King Hrothgar called his workmen and gave them commandment to build the hall. So they set to work, and day by day it rose quickly, becoming each day more and more fair, until at length it was finished.

It stood upon a height, vast and stately, and as it was adorned with the horns of deer, King Hrothgar named it Hart Hall.

Then, true to his word and well pleased with the work of his servants, King Hrothgar made a great feast. To it his warriors young and old were called, and he divided his treasure, giving to each rings of gold.

And so in the Hall there was laughter and song and great merriment. Every evening when the shadows fell, and the land grew dark without, the knights and warriors gathered in the Hall to feast. And when the feast was over, and the wine-cup passed around the board, and the great fire roared upon the hearth, and the dancing flames gleamed and flickered, making strange shadows among the gold and carved work of the walls, the minstrel took his harp and sang.

Then from the many-windowed Hall the light glowed cheerfully. Far over the dreary fen and moorland the gleam was shed, and the sound of song and harp awoke the deep silence of the night.

Within the Hall was light and gladness, but without there was wrath and hate. For far on the moor there lived a wicked giant named Grendel. Hating all joy and brightness, he haunted the fastness and the fen, prowling at night to see what evil he might do.

And now when night by night he heard the minstrel's song, and saw the lighted windows gleam through the darkness, it was pain and grief to him.

Very terrible was this ogre Grendel to look upon. Thick black hair hung about his face, and his teeth were long and sharp, like the tusks of an animal. His huge body and great hairy arms had the strength of ten men. He wore no armour, for his skin was tougher than any coat of mail that man or giant might weld. His nails were like steel and sharper than daggers, and by his side there hung a great pouch in which he carried off those whom he was ready to devour.

Terrible was this ogre Grendel to look upon

Now day by day this fearsome giant was tortured more and more, for to him it was a torture to hear the sounds of laughter and of merriment. Day by day the music of harp and song of minstrel made him more and more mad with jealous hate.

At length he could bear it no longer. Therefore one night he set out, and creeping through the darkness came to Hart Hall, where, after the feast and song were done, the warriors slept.

Peacefully they slept with arms and armour thrown aside, having no fear of any foe. And so with ease the fierce and savage giant seized them with his greedy claws. Speedily he slew thirty of the bravest warriors. Then howling with wicked joy he carried them off to his dark dwelling, there to devour them.

Oh, when morning came, great was the moaning in Daneland. When the sun arose and shone upon the desolated Hall, and the war-craft of Grendel was made plain, there was weeping. A cry of woe and wailing crept out over the moorland, and the woesome sound made glad the heart of the Wicked One.

But Hrothgar, the mighty, sat upon his throne downcast and sorrowful. He who was strong in war wept now for the woe of his thanes.

With eyes dimmed and dark, in grief and rage he looked across the wild wide moorland, where the track of the monster was marked with blood, and he longed for a champion.

But who could fight against an Ogre? Before the thought the bravest quailed. Such a fight would be too loathly, too horrible. It was not to be endured.

When night fell the sorrowing warriors laid themselves down to rest with sighs and tears, in the bright hall that once had rung with songs and laughter. But the greedy monster was not yet satisfied, his work was not yet done. Stealthily through the darkening moorland again the Ogre crept until he reached the Hart Hall.

Again he stretched forth his hand, again he seized the bravest of the warriors, slew and carried them off to his drear dwelling.

Then was there wailing and fierce sorrow among the mighty men. Yet was there none so brave that he would face and fight the demon foe. But each man swore that he would not again sleep beneath the roof of Hart Hall. So when evening fell, they departed every man to the dwellings around the palace, and the fair Hall was left desolate.

Thus Grendel, single handed, warred against the Dane folk until the great Hall, the wonder of men, was forsaken and empty.

For twelve long years it stood thus, no man daring, except in the light of day, to enter it. For after the shadows of evening fell, Grendel was master there. And in that stately Hall, when night was darkest, he held his horrid feasts. Only near to the throne, the carved Gift-seat or throne of the Dane folk, where Hrothgar the king used to sit, and from whence he dispensed gifts to his people, there only he dared not go. Something sacred and pure was there, before which the wicked Ogre trembled.

Thus for twelve long years Grendel warred against Hrothgar and the Dane folk. He prowled through the misty moorland, lay in wait in dark places, slaying young and old. Many were the grisly deeds he did, many the foul crimes. And the mighty warriors, strong of heart against a mortal foe, were powerless against him.

Downcast and sorrowful of heart Hrothgar sat among his counsellors. None among them knew how to give him advice or comfort. None knew how to deliver his land from the Evil One.

Then the minstrels made mournful songs, and far and wide they sang of how Grendel ever warred with Hrothgar. They sang of how year by year there was battle and wrath between the noble King and the Ogre of evil fame.

Chapter II. How Beowulf the Goth Came to Daneland

And now it came to pass that, across the sea in far Gothland, the songs of Grendel and his wrath were sung, until to Beowulf the Goth the tale of woe was carried. And Beowulf, when he heard of Grendel's deeds, cried that he would go across the waves to Hrothgar, the brave king, since he had need of men to help him.

Now Beowulf was very strong in war, mighty among men. Of all the nobles of the Goths there was none so great as he. Much beloved, too, was he of Hygelac, King of the Goths, for they were kinsmen and good comrades. And because of the love they bore him, many prayed him to bide peacefully at home, but others, knowing his prowess, bade him go forth.

Beowulf was eager for the contest, so taking with him fifteen warriors and good comrades, he stepped into a ship and bade the captain set sail for Daneland.

Then like a bird wind-driven upon the waves, the foam-necked ship sped forth. For two days the warriors fared on over the blue sea, until they came again to Daneland and anchored beneath the steep mountains of that far shore.

There, lightly springing to shore, the warriors gave thanks to the sea-god that the voyage had been so short and easy for them.

But upon the heights above them stood the warden of the shore. His duty it was to guard the sea-cliffs and mark well that no foe landed unaware. Now as the warriors sprang to shore, he saw the sun gleam upon sword and shield and coat of mail.

'What manner of men be these?' he asked himself. And mounting upon his horse he rode towards them.

Waving his huge spear aloft, he cried, as he rode onward, 'What men be ye who come thus clad in mail-coats, thus armed with sword and spear? Whence cometh this proud vessel over the waves? Long have I kept watch and ward upon this shore that no foe might come unaware to Daneland, yet never have I seen shield-bearing men come openly as ye. And never have I seen more noble warrior than he who seems your leader. Nay, such splendour of armour, such beauty and grace have I not seen. But, strangers, travellers from the sea, I must know whence ye come ere ye go further. Ye may not pass else, lest ye be spies and enemies to Daneland. It were well that ye told me speedily.'

Then Beowulf answered him, 'We are folk of the Goths, thanes of King Hygelac. In friendly guise we come to seek thy lord, King Hrothgar, the mighty chieftain. We have a goodly message to the famed lord of the Danes. There is no cause to be secret. Thou knowest if it be true or no, but we indeed have heard that among ye Danes there is a great and wily foe, a loather of valour, who prowleth terribly in dark nights, making great slaughter and causing much woe. Therefore have I come, for perchance I may be of succour to the noble King Hrothgar in his need.'

The warriors fared on over the blue sea

Fearless and bold, facing the band of warlike men, the warden sat upon his horse, and when Beowulf had ceased speaking, he answered him.

'Ye come as friends, O bearers of weapons, O wearers of war garments. Follow me then, and I will lead you on. I will also give commandment to my men that they guard your ship where it lies by the shore until ye come again.'

So following the warden they marched forward. Eager they were for battle, eager to see the far-famed Hart Hall. And as they marched, their gold-decked helmets, their steel mail-coats, their jewelled sword-hilts, flashed in the sunlight, and the clank and clash of weapons and armour filled the air.

On and on they pressed quickly, until the warden drew rein. 'There,' he said, pointing onward, 'there lies the great Hart Hall. No longer have ye need of me. The way ye cannot miss. As for me, I will back to the sea to keep watch against a coming foe.'

Then wheeling his horse he galloped swiftly away, while the Goths marched onward until they reached the Hart Hall. There, weary of the long way that they had come, they laid down their shields, and leaning their spears against the walls, sat upon the bench before the great door.

And as they sat there resting, there came to them a proud warrior. 'Whence come ye with these great shields,' he asked, 'whence with these grey shirts of mail, these jewelled helmets and mighty spears? I am Hrothgar's messenger and servant, I who ask. Never saw I prouder strangers, never more seemly men. I ween it is not from some foe ye flee in fear and trouble. Rather in pride and daring it would seem ye come to visit Hrothgar.'

Then answered Beowulf. 'My name is Beowulf, and we are Hygelac's thanes. To thy lord, the mighty Hrothgar, we will tell our errand if he will deign that we do greet him.'

The warrior bowed low, for well he saw that Beowulf was a mighty prince.

'I will ask my lord the King,' he said, 'if so be thou mayest come to him. And to thee right quickly will I bear his answer.'

So saying he departed, and came to Hrothgar where he sat amongst his earls. The king was now old and grey-haired, and sat amid his wise men bowed with grief, for there was none among them mighty enough to free his land from the Ogre.

'My lord,' the warrior said, and knelt before the king, 'from far beyond the sea strange knights are come. They pray that they may speak with thee. These sons of battle name their leader Beowulf. Refuse them not, O king, but give them kindly answer. For by the splendour of their arms I deem them worthy of much honour. The prince who sendeth such warriors hither must be great indeed.'

'Beowulf!' cried Hrothgar. 'I knew him when he was yet a lad. His father and his mother have I known. Truly he hath sought a friend. And I have heard of him that he is much renowned in war, and that he hath the strength of thirty men in the grip of his hand. I pray Heaven he hath been sent to free us from the horror of Grendel. Haste thee, bid him enter, bid them all to come. I would see the whole friendly band together. Say to them that they are right welcome to the land of Danes.'

The warrior bowed low. Then once more going to the door of the Hall, he stood before Beowulf and his knights.

'My lord,' he said, 'the king biddeth me to say to thee that he knoweth already of thy rank and fame. He saith to you brave-hearted men from over the sea that ye are all welcome to him. Now may ye go in to speak with him, wearing your war trappings and with your helmets upon your heads. But leave your shields, your spears, and deadly swords without here, until the talk be done.'

Then Beowulf and his warriors rose. Some went with him to the Hall, others stayed without to guard the shields and weapons.

Guided by the Danish warrior the knights marched right through the great Hart Hall, until they stood before the Gift-seat where sat the aged king.

'Hail to thee, Hrothgar,' cried Beowulf. 'I am Hygelac's friend and kinsman. Many fair deeds have I done though yet I be young. And to me in far Gothland the tales of Grendel's grim warfare were told. Sea-faring men told that the great Hall so fair and well-built doth stand forsaken and empty as soon as the shades of evening fall, because of the prowlings of that fell giant.

'Then as we heard such tales did my friends urge me to come to thee because they knew my might. They had themselves seen how I laid low my foes. Five monsters I bound, thus humbling a giant brood. Sea-monsters I slew in the waves at night-time. Many a wrong have I avenged, fiercely grinding the oppressors.

'And now will I fight against Grendel. Alone against the Ogre will I wage war. Therefore one boon I crave of thee, noble prince. Refuse it not, for thereto am I come from very far. I pray thee that I alone, having with me only mine own earls and comrades, may cleanse Hart Hall.

'It hath been told to me that Grendel recketh not of weapons, for his hide is as of steel armour. Therefore will I bear neither sword nor shield. But I will grapple with the fiend with mine hands alone, and foe to foe we will fight for victory. And, unto whomsoever it seemeth good to the Lord of Life, unto him shall the victory be given.

'If Grendel win, then will he fearlessly devour the people of the Goths my dear comrades, my noble earls, even as aforetime he hath devoured thy warriors. Then wilt thou not need to cover me with a mound, for the lone moor will be my burial-place. Where ye track the footsteps of the Ogre stained with gore, there will he with greed devour my thanes and me.

'But if I die, then send back to Hygelac my coat of mail, for in all the world there is no other like to it. This is all I ask.'

Beowulf was silent, and Hrothgar the aged king answered him.

'O friend Beowulf,' he said, 'thou hast sought us out to help us. Yet to me it is pain and sorrow to tell to any man what shame, what sudden mischiefs, Grendel in his wrath hath done to me. See! my palace-troop, my war-band hath grown small. Grendel hath done this. In his prowlings he hath carried off my men so that my warriors are few.

'Full oft when the wine was red in the cup my knights did swear that they would await the coming of Grendel, to meet him with sword-thrust. So when night fell they abode in the Hall. But in the morning, when day dawned, my fair house was red with blood. And I needs must mourn the death of yet more gallant knights, must have fewer thanes to own my rule.

'But sit now to the feast and eat with gladness, sure that victory will come to thee.'

So the Goths sat them down in the great Hart Hall and feasted with the Dane folk. The mead cup was carried round, the minstrel sang of deeds of love and battle, and there was great joy and laughter in all the Hall.

Chapter III. Beowulf Telleth How He Warred with the Sea-Folk

Now among all the joyous company who feasted and made merry in the Hart Hall there was one who bore a gloomy face and angry heart. This was a knight named Hunferth. At Hrothgar's feet he sat in jealous wrath, for he could not bear that any knight in all the world should have greater fame than he himself. The praise of Beowulf was bitterness to him, and thus he spake in scoffing words:

'Art thou that Beowulf who didst contend with Breca on the wide sea in a swimming match? Art thou he who with Breca, out of vain pride swam through the sea, and for foolhardiness ventured your lives in deep waters? No man, 'twas said, nor friend nor foe could turn ye from the foolish play. 'Twas winter-time and the waves dashed with loud fury. Yet for a week ye twain strove upon the waters.

'He overcame thee in swimming, he had more strength. Then at morning-time the sea drave him to shore. Thence he departed to his own land where he owned a nation, a town, and much wealth. Yea, in that contest thou hadst not the better. Now although thou art so splendid in war, I expect a worse defeat for thee, if thou darest to abide here the coming of Grendel.'

'Friend Hunferth,' said Beowulf quietly, 'thou hast spoken much of Breca and of our contest. Now will I tell thee the truth of the matter. Rightly I claim to have the greatest strength upon the sea, more skill than any man upon the waves.

'Breca and I when we were boys talked much thereon, and swore that when we were grown to men we should venture our lives upon the sea. And even so we did.

'As we swam forth into the waves, our naked swords we held in hand. That was right needful to defend us against the whale-fishes.

'Breca was not fleeter than I upon the waves. Strive as he might, he could not flee from me. And so for five nights upon the sea we swam. Then a great storm arose and drave us asunder. Fierce and cold were the waves, dark and terrible the night. The north wind drave upon us till the ocean boiled in madness of wrath.

'Then too the anger of the sea-monsters arose. Glad was I then that my shirt of mail, gold adorned and trusty, wrapped my body. For a spotted monster seized me fast in his grim grip and dragged me to the floor of the sea. But I strove with him and my bright blade was dyed in the blood of the sea-brute.

'So I escaped me that time. Yet, although one was slain, around me swarmed many another fearful foe. But my dear sword served me well. They did not have joy of their feast, the Evil-doers! They did not sit around on the floor of the sea to swallow me down. Nay rather, in the morning, put to sleep with the sword, they lay among the sea-weeds on the shore, cast up by the waves. And never since upon the great waters have they troubled the sailors.

'Yea, in that contest I slew nine sea-brutes. Never have I heard of a fiercer fight by night under the arch of heaven. Never have I heard of a man more wretched upon the waves. Yet I escaped. And when the sun at morning rose above the sea, the waves cast me upon the shore of Finland, spent and weary of my journey.

'I have never heard it said that thou, Hunferth, didst make such play of sword, no nor Breca, nor any of you. Ye have not done such deeds. But in sooth I would not boast myself. Yet I say unto thee, Hunferth, that Grendel, the evil monster, had never done so many horrors against thy king, that he had never brought such shame upon this fair Hall, hadst thou been so battle-fierce as thou vauntest that thou art. Yea, he hath seen that he hath no need to fear the boasted courage of the Dane folk. So he warreth, and slayeth, and feasteth as he pleaseth. He looketh not for battle at the hands of the Danes. But I, a Goth, shall offer him war, war fierce and long. And after that, he who will may go proudly to Hart Hall.'

When Beowulf had ceased speaking there was a cry from all the thanes and earls. The Hall rang with the sound of clashing armour and loud shouts as the Dane folk cheered the hero.

But Hunferth abashed held his peace.

Then forth from the bower came Wealtheow, Hrothgar's queen. Stately and tall, and very beautiful she came, clothed in rich garments girdled with gold. A golden crown was upon her head, and jewels glittered upon her neck. In her hand she held a great golden cup set with gems. First to King Hrothgar she went and gave to him the beaker.

'Hail to thee,' she cried, 'mayest thou have joy of the drinking, joy of the feast, ever dear to thy people.'

And Hrothgar drank, merry of heart, glad with thoughts of the morrow.

Then through all the Hall Wealtheow moved, speaking gracious words, giving to each warrior, young and old, wine from the golden cup. At last she, the crowned queen, courteous and beautiful, came to Beowulf.

Giving to each warrior, young and old, wine from the golden cup

Graciously Wealtheow smiled upon the Goth lord, holding the beaker to him.

'I thank the Lord of All, that thou art come to us,' she said. 'Thou art come, noble earl, to bring us comfort, and to deliver us out of our sorrows.'

The fierce warrior bowed before the beautiful queen, as he held the wine-cup. He felt the joy of battle rise within him, and aloud he spake:

'I sware it when I did set out upon the deep sea, as I stood by my comrades upon the ship. I sware that I alone would do the deed or go down to death in the grip of the monster. As an earl I must fulfil my word, or here in the Hart Hall must I await my death-day.'

The queen was well pleased with the proud words of the Goth lord. And so in splendour and high state she moved through the Hall till she came again to the Gift-seat, and there beside the king she sat.

Then again in the Hall there was sound of laughter and merriment. The minstrels sang, and the earls told of mighty deeds until the evening shadows slanted along the wall. Then all arose. The sound of song and laughter was stilled. It was time to be gone.

Farewells were said. Man greeted man, not knowing what the morning might bring forth. But all knew that battle was making ready for those who waited in that great Hall. When the sun had gone down, and dark night covered all the land, ghostly creatures would creep forth to war in the shadow.

So with grave words Hrothgar bade Beowulf farewell.

'Good luck bide with thee,' he said. 'Into thy keeping I give the Hall of the Dane folk. Never before did I commit it to any man. Keep it now right bravely. Remember thy fame, show thy great valour, and watch against the Evil-doer. If thou overcome him, there is no desire of thine that shall be unfulfilled, so that it lieth in my power to give it thee.'

Then Hrothgar and his band of warriors and thanes went forth from the Hall, and Beowulf with his comrades was left to guard it.

The beds were spread around the walls, and Beowulf prepared himself strangely for battle. His coat of mail, firmly wrought with shining rings of steel, he cast aside. He took his helmet from his head, and with his sword and shield, and all his glittering war-harness, gave it to the keeping of a servant.

And thus all unarmed, clad only in his silken coat, he proudly spake:

'In war-craft I deem I am no worse than Grendel. Therefore not with the sword shall I put him to sleep, though that were easy. Not thus shall I take his life, for he is not learned in the use of war-weapons. So without them we twain this night shall fight. And God the all-wise shall give victory even as it shall seem best to Him.'

Having so spoken Beowulf laid his head upon his pillow and all around him his warriors lay down to take their rest. None among them thought ever again to see his own land. For they had heard of the terrible death that had carried off so many of the Dane folk from Hart Hall. Little they thought to escape that death. Yet so reckless were they of life that soon they slept. They who were there to guard that high Hall slept—all save one.

Beowulf alone, watchful and waiting for the foe, impatiently longed for the coming battle.

Chapter IV. How Beowulf Overcame Grendel the Ogre

And now all slept save Beowulf alone. Then out of the creeping mists that covered the moorland forth the Evil Thing strode.

Right onward to the Hall he came, goaded with fearful wrath. The bolts and bars he burst asunder with but a touch, and stood within the Hall.

Out of the dark Grendel's eyes blazed like fire. Loud he laughed, wild-demon laughter, as he gazed around upon the sleeping warriors.

Here truly was a giant feast spread out before him. And ere morning light should come he meant to leave no man of them alive. So loud he laughed.

Beowulf, watchful and angry, yet curbed his wrath. He waited to see how the monster should attack. Nor had he long to wait.

Quickly stretching forth a fang, Grendel seized a sleeping warrior. Ere the unhappy one could wake he was torn asunder. Greedily Grendel drank his blood, crushed his bones, and swallowed his horrid feast.

Again the goblin stretched forth his claws hungry for his feast. But Beowulf raising himself upon his elbow reached out his hand, and caught the monster.

Then had the fell giant fierce wrath and pain. Never before had he made trial of such a hand-grip. In it he writhed and struggled vainly. Hotter and hotter grew his anger, deeper and deeper his fear. He longed to flee, to seek his demon lair and there make merry with his fellows. But though his strength was great he could not win free from that mighty grasp.

Then Beowulf, remembering his boast that he would conquer this ruthless beast, stood upright, gripping the Ogre yet more firmly.

Awful was the fight in the darkness. This way and that the Ogre swayed, but he could not free himself from the clutch of those mighty fingers.

The noise of the contest was as of thunder. The fair Hall echoed and shook with demon cries of rage, until it seemed that the walls must fall.

The wine in the cups was spilled upon the floor. The benches, overlaid with gold, were torn from their places. Fear and wonder fell upon the Dane folk. For far and wide the din was heard, until the king trembled in his castle, the slave in his hut.

The knights of Beowulf awoke, arose, drew their sharp swords, and plunged into the battle. They fought right manfully for their master, their great leader. But though they dealt swift and mighty blows, it was in vain. Grendel's hide was such that not the keenest blade ever wrought of steel could pierce it through. No war-axe could wound him, for by enchantments he had made him safe. Nay, by no such honourable means might death come to the foul Ogre.

Louder and louder grew the din, fiercer and wilder the strife, hotter the wrath of those who strove.

But at length the fight came to an end. The sinews in Grendel's shoulder burst, the bones cracked. Then the Ogre tore himself free, and fled, wounded to death, leaving his arm in Beowulf's mighty grip.

Sobbing forth his death-song, Grendel fled over the misty moorland, until he reached his dwelling in the lake of the Water Dragons, and there plunged in. The dark waves closed over him, and he sank to his home.

Loud were the songs of triumph in Hart Hall, great the rejoicing. For Beowulf had made good his boast. He had cleansed the Hall from the Ogre. Henceforth might the Dane folk sleep peacefully therein. And so the Goths rejoiced. And over the doorway of the Hall, in token of his triumph, Beowulf nailed the hand, and arm, and shoulder of Grendel.

Then when morning came, and the news was spread over all the land, there was much joy among the Dane folk. From far and near many a warrior came riding to the Hall to see the marvel. Over the moor they rode, too, tracking Grendel's gory footsteps, until they came to the lake of the Water Dragons. There they gazed upon the water as it boiled and seethed, coloured dark with the poison blood of the Ogre.

Then back with light hearts they sped, praising the hero. 'From north to south,' they cried, 'between the seas all the world over, there is none so valiant as he, none so worthy of honour.'

With loosened rein they galloped in the gay sunshine. And by the way minstrels made songs, and sang of the mighty deeds of the Goth hero, praising him above the heroes of old. In all the land there was song and gladness.

Then from his bower came the aged king, clad in gorgeous robes. Behind him was his treasurer, the keeper of his gold, and a great troop of warriors. With him walked the queen, splendid too, in robes of purple and gold, while many fair ladies followed in her train.

Over the flower-starred meadow they passed, stately and beautiful, until they stood before the Hall.

As Hrothgar mounted the steps, he gazed upon the roof shining with gold in the sun. He gazed too upon the hand and arm of Grendel. Great was his joy and gladness.

Then the king turned to the people gathered there. 'For this sight be thanks at once given to the All Wise,' he cried. 'What sorrow and trouble hath Grendel caused me! When I saw my Hall stained with blood, when I saw my wise men bowed with grief, broken in spirit, I hoped no more. I thought never in this life to be repaid for all the brave men that I have lost.

'Then lo! when my sorrow was dark, there cometh a young warrior, a youth mighty in battle. And he hath done the deed that all our wisdom was not able to perform.'

Then turning to Beowulf, the king stretched out his hands and cried, 'Now, O Beowulf, greatest of fighters, henceforth will I love thee as a son. No wish of thine but I will grant it to thee, if it be in my power.

'Full oft of yore have I for lesser deeds given great rewards. Treasure and honour have I heaped upon knights less brave than thou, less mighty in war. But thou by thy deeds hast made for thyself a glorious name which shall never be forgotten.'

Then Beowulf, proudly humble, answered, 'It was joy to do the daring deed. Blithe at heart we fought the Unknown One. But I would that thou thyself hadst seen the Ogre among the treasures of the Hall. I thought to bind him on a bed of death. But in my hand he might not lie. He was too strong for me. His body slipped from my grasp. Nevertheless he left with me his hand and arm and shoulder. It is certain that now he lieth dead and will never more trouble the land.'

There was joy among the heroes as Beowulf spoke. But Hunferth hung his head, and bit his lip in silence. He no longer had desire to taunt the hero, or make boast of his own war-craft. Shame held him speechless.

And so through all that day the crowd came and went before the door of Hart Hall. Greatly did all men marvel at the fearful sight, at the war-hand of the Ogre. The nails were like steel, the fingers like daggers, and the whole hide so hard that no sword, however finely welded, might pierce it through.

It was indeed a great marvel.

Chapter V. How the Water Witch Warred with the Dane Folk

And now while the people came and went, marvelling and praising the skill of him who had overcome the Goblin, men and women hurried hither and thither making gay the Hall.

The carving and gem work was much broken and destroyed by the fearful combat which had taken place within. The roof alone was quite unhurt. But beautiful tapestries gleaming with gold and colours were hung upon the walls, silken banners and embroideries were spread upon the benches, until the whole Hall glowed in splendour.

Then came the king with all his knights and nobles to the great feast which was prepared. Never was there more splendid banquet. Hart Hall from end to end was filled with friends, and laughter, and rejoicing sounded through it.

Then when the feasting was over Hrothgar gave to Beowulf rich presents. A splendid banner he gave him richly sewed with gold, a helmet and coat of mail, a sword the hilt of which was all of twisted gold.

Eight splendid horses, too, were led into the court about the Hall. Their harness was all of gold, and upon one was a saddle gaily decorated and finely adorned with silver. It was the saddle upon which Hrothgar himself rode when he went forth to battle.

All these the king gave to Beowulf, and much wealth besides.

And to his companions also, to the mighty heroes who were with their master, great treasure was given of swords and gold. Also for the man whom Grendel had slain Hrothgar ordered that much gold should be paid.

Then when the present-giving was over, the minstrel took his harp and sang. He sang of love and battle, and of the mighty deeds of heroes.

The singing ceased, and the noise of laughter and merriment burst forth once more. Around the board the cup-bearers carried the wine in vessels wondrously wrought.

Then came Queen Wealtheow forth once more, clad in splendid robes, wearing a golden crown upon her head, bearing in her hand a golden cup.

To the king she went where he sat with his sons and Beowulf beside him.

'Accept this cup, my beloved Lord,' she said, 'and be thou happy. Far and near now hast thou peace. Hart Hall is cleansed of the Evil One.'

Then to Beowulf she turned bearing the cup to him with friendly words. At his feet she laid a rich dress with bracelets and a collar of fine gold.

'Take this collar, dear Beowulf,' she said, 'and this mantle. Long mayest thou wear them and enjoy life. A deed hast thou done this night that shall be remembered for all time. Far as the seas circle the land shall it be told of thee. Take thou my thanks, and be thou a friend to my sons.'

Then the queen went again to her place and sat beside the king.

Once more there was song and laughter throughout the Hall until the shadows of evening fell. Then the king and Beowulf arose, and went forth to rest, each to his own chamber. But the Dane lords, as they had done so often before in days gone by, spread their beds and pillows upon the floor of the great Hall. For now that the Ogre was dead they had no more fear.

At the head of his bed each man placed his shield. Upon the bench near him stood his helmet, his sword and spear and coat of mail. Then each man lay down to rest secure and happy. For was not the terrible giant slain? No more was there need to watch and fear.

So silence and darkness fell upon the Hall, and all men sank to sleep.

But out on the wide moorland, far away in the Water Dragon's lake, there was one who waked and mourned. Over the dead body of her son Grendel's mother wept, desiring revenge.

Very terrible was this Water Witch to look upon. Almost as fearful as her wicked son she was. And as the darkness fell upon the land she crept forth across the moorland to Hart Hall.

On and on she crept until she reached the door. Then in she rushed among the sleeping warriors, eager for slaughter. The fear and confusion were great. A wild cry rang through the Hall, and each man sprang to his feet seizing his sword and shield.

Then the Water Witch, finding herself discovered, made haste to be gone. No mind had she to face these swords and spears. But ere she went she stretched forth her hand and seized a warrior, and tightly holding him, she carried him off to the moor. And though her haste to be gone was great she found yet time to seize the hand of Grendel and take it with her to her dark dwelling.

Great was the sound of woe throughout the Hall. For the warrior whom the Water Witch had carried off was a dear comrade of the king. He was the best beloved of all Hrothgar's thanes.

Now when messengers came running in all haste to the old king with the direful news, he was filled with grief and anger. His joy at the death of Grendel was all dashed with grief for the loss of his friend.

'Oh that Beowulf had been there,' he moaned.

Then all men's thoughts turned to Beowulf. Quickly they ran to fetch him, and he, waked thus suddenly out of his sleep, came with his comrades wonderingly to the king where he awaited them.

The sun had not yet risen, and all the Hall was dim in grey shadow, as Beowulf and his men marched through it, breaking the stillness with the clang of their weapons and armour.

'My lord king,' said Beowulf, as he reached the Gift-seat, 'hath the night not passed fair and pleasantly with thee? Is some evil chance befallen that thy messengers seek me thus early?'

Hrothgar leaned his head upon his hand and sighed.

'Ask not thou of happiness,' he moaned. 'Sorrow is renewed to the Dane folk. My dearest comrade is dead, my friend and counsellor. Thou didst slay Grendel yesternight, but one hath come to avenge him, even his mother. She it is who hath carried off my dear warrior to slay and devour him in her dwelling.

'Scarce a mile hence lieth that grim lake. Dank trees overshadow it and no man knoweth its depth, for all shun the gloomy place. Yet if thou durst, seek it out. Rid me of this Water Witch, avenge there the death of my comrade, and with treasure and twisted gold will I reward thee,' and overcome with grief Hrothgar ceased from speaking.

'Sorrow not, O king,' replied Beowulf. 'It is ever better to avenge than to grieve for one's friend. To each of us must death come, and well for him then who hath done justice while he yet lived. Arise, O king, let us see quickly the track of Grendel's kin. I promise thee she shall not escape. Do thou but have patience this day, that only do I ask of thee.'

Then up sprang the aged king. 'May the gods be praised,' he cried, 'who have sent me such a man.'

Quickly he gave orders that horses should be brought, and mounting, he rode forth with Beowulf. After them came a great train of warriors as across the moor they went, following the track of the Water Witch to her home.

By rocky gorges and lonely ways over the murky moor they went, following always the gory track of the foe. At length they came to the place where gloomy trees hung over red and troubled waters. Upon the bank lay the head of that Dane warrior, Hrothgar's dear friend, and at the sight of it the knights were again filled with woe.

Upon the dark water there swam strange Sea Dragons, many kinds of snakes and savage worms. But when they saw the company of Danes upon the bank, and heard the blast of the war-horn, they fled swimming away, diving into the depths.

Yet ere they vanished Beowulf drew his bow and shot one of them. Then quickly with boar-spears and hooks the warriors drew him to land, and as he lay there dead they gazed in wonder upon the grisly monster.

And now once more did Beowulf prepare himself for battle. He wore his trusty coat of steel, and upon his head was a wondrously wrought helmet, through which no sword might bite.

Then as Beowulf made ready, Hunferth came to him. In his hand he bare an ancient and famous sword named Hrunting. The edge of it was stained with poisonous twigs and hardened in gore. Never had it failed a man, who carrying it went forth to ways of terror and war. Many valiant deeds had it wrought.

And now Hunferth, remembering how he had taunted Beowulf, and in sorrow at the memory, brought the famous sword to the Goth hero.

Hunferth himself durst not venture his life amid the waves to do the deed, and thus fame was lost to him. But he was now eager to aid Beowulf. And the Goth, who thought no longer of Hunferth's taunting words, received the sword right gladly.

Then Beowulf turned to King Hrothgar. 'I am ready, O prince,' he said, 'for my journey. Let me but first call to thy mind what we have already spoken. If I for thy need lose my life, be thou a friend to my fellow-thanes. And do thou also send the treasure which thou hast given unto me to my king, Hygelac. Then by that gold may he know that I did fight manfully, and found in thee a noble rewarder.

'But to Hunferth I pray thee to give the curious war-sword which is among thy gifts, for he is a right noble warrior. With his Hrunting I will work renown, or death shall take me.'

Then, waiting for no answer, Beowulf plunged into the dark lake and was lost to sight.

Chapter VI. How Beowulf Overcame the Water Witch

Down and down and down Beowulf dived. It seemed to him that he dived for a whole day's space ere he reached the bottom of that dark lake.

But as soon as he touched the water, the grim and greedy Water Witch knew by the movement of the waves that a mortal man was coming. So she made ready to seize the daring one in her horrid clutches.

No sooner then did Beowulf near the bottom than he was grasped by long and skinny fingers. The fingers crushed him, and tore at him, but so strong and trusty was his coat of mail that the Water Witch could in no wise hurt him.

Then seeing that she could not so easily as she had hoped harm him, she dragged him into her dwelling. And so fast was Beowulf in her clutches that he could not unsheath his sword.

As the Water Witch dragged Beowulf along, wondrous sea-brutes followed them. Beasts they were with terrible tusks, shining scales and sharp fins. With these they attacked the hero so fiercely that his armour was rent, yet was he unwounded.

At last the Water Witch reached a great cave. Here there was no water, and a fire burned with a strange weird flame, lighting up the vast dim place.

Then by the pale light of the goblin fire Beowulf saw that it was no other than Grendel's mother, the Water Witch, who held him. And he knew that the time for battle had come.

With a mighty effort he wrenched himself free. Then drawing the sword Hrunting which Hunferth had given him, he dealt with it many great blows. But all his strength was vain. Hrunting, so famous in many battles, was useless against the Water Witch. No harm could the warrior do to her.

Then in wrath Beowulf threw the shining blade upon the ground. He would trust no more in weapons but with his hands alone would he fight.

She bore him to the ground and kneeled upon his breast

Seizing the Water Witch by the shoulders, he dragged her downwards. But she grappled with him fiercely. Then was there a fearful fight in that dim hall, deep under the water, far from all hope of help.

Back and forth the two swayed, the strong warrior in armour and the direful Water Witch. So strong was she that at last she bore him to the ground and kneeled upon his breast. She drew her dagger. Now she would avenge her son, her only son.

The dagger shone and fell again and yet again. And then truly Beowulf's last hour had come had his armour not been of such trusty steel. But through it neither point nor edge of dagger might pierce. The blows of the Water Witch were all in vain, and again Beowulf sprang to his feet.

And now among the many weapons with which the walls were hung, Beowulf saw a huge sword. It seemed the work of giants. Its edge was keen and bright, the hilt of glittering gold.

Quickly Beowulf grasped the mighty weapon. And now fighting for his very life he swung it fiercely, and smote with fury.

Down upon the floor sank the Water Witch, and from the red-dyed blade a sudden flame shone out, and all the cave was lighted up.

Curiously Beowulf gazed around him. Dead at his feet lay the Water Witch, and hard by on a couch lay the body of Grendel.

Then Beowulf was minded to bear away with him some prize. So once more swinging the great sword, he smote off the Ogre's head.

Meanwhile far up above beyond the water-waves Hrothgar and his men and all Beowulf's comrades sat waiting and watching. And now as Beowulf smote off Grendel's head they saw the waves all dyed with blood.

Then the old men shook their heads and spoke together. They talked sadly of the brave champion who had gone alone beneath that awful water. For now that they saw the waves red-dyed they had no longer hope that he would ever return. Nay, these red and turgid waters seemed to prove to them that the Water Witch had overcome Beowulf and torn him in pieces.

So as the hours passed, and Beowulf came no more, Hrothgar arose, and he and all his warriors sadly wended their way homeward. Nevermore did they hope to see the hero.

But Beowulf's comrades would not go. Sad at heart they sat by the lake's edge gazing into the water, wishing, but hardly hoping, that they might see their dear lord again.

And now far beneath the dark waves a strange thing happened. As Beowulf struck off the head of Grendel, the great sword began to melt away. More quickly than ice when the thaw is come melted the shining steel, until there was nothing left but the golden hilt which Beowulf held in his hand. Such was the poison of the Ogre's blood.

Beowulf gazed in wonder at the miracle. Then he made haste to be gone. All around him lay great treasure. Gold and gems gleamed in the pale firelight. Yet of it all Beowulf took nothing save the hilt of the sword wherewith he had slain the Water Witch.

Hunferth's sword, Hrunting, he once more hung at his side, then, with the grisly head of Grendel in his hand, he dived up through the waves. And as he swam through it, all the water was made pure and clear again, for the power of the grim Ogre was over for ever.

Long time Beowulf swam upwards, but at last he reached the surface and sprang to land. Then round him, greatly rejoicing, crowded his thanes. Quickly they loosed his helmet and coat of mail, and joyed to find that he had suffered no hurt.

They carried with them the hideous head of Grendel

Then right merrily they turned back to Hart Hall. With them they carried the hideous head of Grendel, which was so huge and heavy that it had need of four of them to bear it. Yet gladly they bore it, rejoicing as they went at the return of their master.

Chapter VII. How Beowulf Returned to His Own Land

Proudly the Goths marched along with Beowulf in their midst, until they reached Hart Hall. And there, still carrying the hideous head of Grendel, they entered in and greeted Hrothgar.

Great was the astonishment of the king and his nobles at the sight of Beowulf. Never again had they thought to see the daring warrior. So now they welcomed him with much rejoicing, and their rejoicing was mingled with wonder and awe as they gazed upon the awful head. The queen, too, who sat beside the king, turned from it with a shudder.

Then when the noise of joyful greeting was stilled a little, Beowulf spoke.

'Behold, O king!' he said, 'we bring thee these offerings in token of victory. From the conflict under the water have I hardly escaped with my life. Had not the All-wise shielded me, I had nevermore seen the sun and the joyful light of day. For although Hrunting be a mighty and good sword, in this fight it availed me nothing. So I cast it from me and fought with mine hands only.

'But the Water Witch was strong and evil, and I had but little hope of life, when it chanced that I saw on the walls there of that grim cave an old and powerful sword.

'Quickly then I drew that weapon and therewith slew I the dreadful foe. After that I espied the body of Grendel which lay there and cut off his head, which now I bring to thee. But even as I had done that, lo! a marvel happened, and the blade did melt even as ice under the summer sun. Such was the venom of that Ogre's blood, that the hilt only of the sword have I borne away with me.

'But now, I promise thee, henceforth mayest thou and thy company of warriors sleep safe in Hart Hall. No longer will the Demon folk trouble it.'

Then Beowulf gave the golden hilt to the king, and he, taking it, gazed on it in wonder. It was exceeding ancient and of marvellous workmanship, a very treasure. Upon the gold of it in curious letters was written for whom that sword had been first wrought. The writing told, too, how it had been made in days long past, when giants stalked the earth in pride.

In the Hall there was silence as Hrothgar gazed upon the relic. Then in the silence he spoke.

'Thy glory is exalted through wide ways, O friend Beowulf,' he said. 'Over every nation thy fame doth spread. Yet thou bearest it modestly, true warrior-like. Again I renew my plighted love to thee, and to thine own people mayest thou long be a joy.

'I for half a hundred years had ruled my folk, and under all the wide heaven there was no foe who stood against me. Within my borders there was peace and joy. Then lo, after joy came sadness, and Grendel became my foe, my invader. But thanks be to the Eternal Lord I am yet in life to see that fearful head besprent with gore.

'And now, O Great-in-war, go thou to thy seat, enjoy the feast, and when it shall be morning, thou and I shall deal together in many treasures.'

Then at these words Beowulf was glad at heart, and went straightway to his seat as the king commanded. And once again the

Dane folk and the Goths feasted together in merry mood.

At length the day grew dim and darkness fell upon the land. All the courtiers then rose, and the grey-bearded king sought his couch. Beowulf, too, rejoiced greatly at the thought of rest, for he was weary with his long contest. So the king's servants, with every honour and reverence, guided him to the room prepared for him.

Silence and peace descended upon the Hall and palace. Hour after hour the night passed, and no demon foe disturbed the sleep of Goth or Dane.

And when the morning sun shone again the Goths arose, eager to see their own land once more.

Beowulf then called one of his thanes and bade him bear the famous sword, Hrunting, back again to Hunferth. Great thanks he gave for it, nor spoke he word of blame against the good blade. 'Nay, 'twas a good war friend,' said the high-souled warrior.

Then, impatient to depart, with arms all ready, the Goths came to bid King Hrothgar farewell.

'Now to thee we sea-farers would bid farewell,' said Beowulf, 'for we would seek again our own king, Hygelac. Here have we been kindly served. Thou hast entreated us well. If I can now do aught more of warlike works on thy behalf, O Hrothgar, I am straightway ready. If from far over the sea I hear that to thy dwelling foes come again, I will bring thousands of warriors to thine aid.

'For well I know that Hygelac, King of the Goths, young though he be, will help me to fight for thee, and will not refuse his thanes.'

With gracious words the old king thanked the young warrior. Rich presents, too, he gave to him, of gold and gems, and splendidly wrought armour. Then he bade him seek his own people, but come again right speedily.

As Hrothgar said farewell he put his arms round Beowulf's neck and kissed him. Then as he watched the hero march away across the fields of summer green, his eyes filled with tears. It was to the king as if he parted from a beloved son.

Proudly and gladly the Goths marched on until they came to the shore where the warden watched who had met them at their first landing. Now as he saw them come he rode towards them with words of welcome. For already the tale of Beowulf's great deeds had been told to him.

And thus at length the Goths reached their ship where it lay by the shore awaiting their coming. Into it was piled all the treasure with which Hrothgar had loaded the heroes. The horses were led on board, the glittering shields were hung along the sides, the sails were spread.

Then from out his treasure hoard Beowulf chose a splendid sword and gave it to the thane who had watched by the ship, and kept it safe. And he, greatly rejoicing, departed to his fellows, and was by them ever after held in honour by reason of the sword that Beowulf had given to him.

Now at length all was ready. The last man leaped on board, the sails shook themselves to the wind, and out upon the waves floated the foam-necked vessel.

Bounding over the sea went the Goths, listening to the song of the wind and the waves, until they came to the shore of their beloved land.

The ship touched the shore. Right joyously the warriors sprang to earth, greeting their kinsmen who welcomed them from the far land.

Beowulf then bade his servants bring the great load of treasure, while he and his comrades set out along the sandy shore to Hygelac's palace.

Quickly before them ran messengers bearing to the king the joyous news that Beowulf, his loved comrade, had returned alive and unhurt. Unwounded from the game of war he had returned, and was even now marching towards the palace.

Gladly the king greeted the hero; joyful words he spake. Then he made Beowulf to sit beside him while Hygd, his fair queen, bare the mead-cup through the hall.

Hygelac was eager to hear all that had befallen his friend. 'Tell it unto me,' he cried, 'how befell it with thee on the way, dear Beowulf? How hath it fared with thee since thou didst on a sudden resolve to seek conflict afar? Sorrow and care have possessed my mind. I have grieved for thee, my friend, lest evil should come to thee. Therefore this day I thank the All-wise that I see thee safe and whole.'

'It is no secret, my Lord Hygelac,' answered Beowulf, 'how I met and overcame the Ogre. None of Grendel's kinsmen who may yet dwell upon earth have any cause to boast of that twilight meeting.'

And then from the beginning of the adventure to the end of it Beowulf told. Sitting beside the king he told of all that had befallen him and his comrades since first they set sail from Gothland. He told of the friendly greeting of the king, of the fight with Grendel, and with Grendel's mother, the foul Water Witch. And at last he told of all the rewards and thanks that had been heaped upon him.

To all the tale Hygelac listened with wonder and delight, for he joyed to hear of the great deeds of his loved comrade.

When Beowulf had finished telling the tale, he bade his servants bring in the treasure. Then turning to the king he spoke again.

'To thee, O warrior-king,' he said, 'I gladly give these riches. For all my joy in life cometh from thee. Save thee, O Hygelac, few kinsmen have I.'

Then to the king he gave a splendid suit of armour, helmet and sword, four steeds all with their rich harness, and much treasure beside.

To Hygd, the queen, Beowulf gave the collar which Wealtheow had bestowed upon him. Also he gave to her three black steeds saddled and harnessed with gold and silver work.

And the king, on his part, gave Beowulf a sword of honour, a palace, and much land. Thus was the mighty warrior brought to great honour.

Then for many years Beowulf lived happy and beloved. For although he was strong and mighty in battle, he was gentle and courteous in peace. His was no savage soul delighting in slaughter; he held himself ever in battle but as a good soldier should.

Indeed Beowulf was so gentle in peace that in his youth the great warriors of the Goths had thought little of him. But now that he had proved that though in peace his words were smooth, in battle his arm was strong, all men honoured him.

And thus it befell that when Hygelac died in battle, and afterward his son also, the broad realm of Gothland was given unto Beowulf to rule. And there for fifty years he reigned a well-loved king, and all the land had peace.

Chapter VIII. How the Fire Dragon Warred with the Goth Folk

And now when many years had come and gone and the realm had long time been at peace, sorrow came upon the people of the Goths. And thus it was that the evil came.

It fell upon a time that a slave by his misdeeds roused his master's wrath, and when his lord would have punished him he fled in terror. And as he fled trembling to hide himself, he came by chance into a great cave.

There the slave hid, thankful for refuge. But soon he had cause to tremble in worse fear than before, for in the darkness of the cave he saw that a fearful dragon lay asleep. Then as the slave gazed in terror at the awful beast, he saw that it lay guarding a mighty treasure.

Never had he seen such a mass of wealth. Swords and armour inlaid with gold, cups and vessels of gold and silver set with precious stones, rings and bracelets lay piled around in glittering heaps.

For hundreds of years this treasure had lain there in secret. A great prince had buried it in sorrow for his dead warriors. In his land there had been much fighting until he alone of all his people was left. Then in bitter grief he gathered all his treasure and hid it in this cave.

'Take, O earth,' he cried, 'what the heroes might not keep. Lo! good men and true once before earned it from thee. Now a warlike death hath taken away every man of my people. There is none now to bear the sword or receive the cup. There is no more joy in the battlefield or in the hall of peace. So here shall the gold-adorned helmet moulder, here the coat of mail rust and the wine-cup lie empty.'

Thus the sad prince mourned. Beside his treasure he sat weeping both day and night until death took him also, and of all his people there was none left.

So the treasure lay hidden and secret for many a day.

Then upon a time it happened that a great Dragon, fiery-eyed and fearful, as it flew by night and prowled seeking mischief, came upon the buried hoard.

As men well know, a dragon ever loveth gold. So to guard his new-found wealth lest any should come to rob him of it, he laid him down there and the cave became his dwelling. Thus for three hundred years he lay gloating over his treasure, no man disturbing him.

But now at length it chanced that the fleeing slave lighted upon the hoard. His eyes were dazzled by the shining heap. Upon it lay a cup of gold, wondrously chased and adorned.

'If I can but gain that cup,' said the slave to himself, 'I will return with it to my master, and for the sake of the gold he will surely forgive me.'

So while the Dragon slept, trembling and fearful the slave crept nearer and nearer to the glittering mass. When he came quite near he reached forth his hand and seized the cup. Then with it he fled back to his master.

It befell then as the slave had foreseen. For the sake of the wondrous cup his misdeeds were forgiven him.

But when the Dragon awoke his fury was great. Well knew he that mortal man had trod his cave and stolen of his hoard.

Round and round about he sniffed and searched until he discovered the footprints of his foe. Eagerly then all over the ground he sought to find the man who, while he slept, had done him this ill. Hot and fierce of mood he went backwards and forwards round about his treasure-heaps. All within the cave he searched in vain. Then coming forth he searched without. All round the hill in which his cave was he prowled, but no man could he find, nor in all the wilds around was there any man.

Again the old Dragon returned, again he searched among his treasure-heaps for the precious cup. Nowhere was it to be found. It was too surely gone.

But the Dragon, as well as loving gold, loved war. So now in angry mood he lay couched in his lair. Scarce could he wait until darkness fell, such was his wrath. With fire he was resolved to repay the loss of his dear drinking-cup.

At last, to the joy of the great winged beast, the sun sank. Then forth from his cave he came, flaming fire.

Spreading his mighty wings, he flew through the air until he came to the houses of men. Then spitting forth flame, he set fire to many a happy homestead. Wherever the lightning of his tongue struck, there fire flamed forth, until where the fair homes of men had been there was nought but blackened ruins. Here and there, this way and that, through all the land he sped, and wherever he passed fire flamed aloft.

The warfare of the Dragon was seen from far. The malice of the Worm was known from north to south, from east to west. All men knew how the fearful foe hated and ruined the Goth folk.

The slave crept nearer and nearer to the glittering mass

Then having worked mischief and desolation all night through, the Fire-Dragon turned back; to his secret cave he slunk again ere break of day. Behind him he left the land wasted and desolate.

The Dragon had no fear of the revenge of man. In his fiery warfare he trusted to find shelter in his hill, and in his secret cave. But in that trust he was misled.

Speedily to King Beowulf were the tidings of the Dragon and his spoiling carried. For alas! even his own fair palace was wrapped in flame. Before his eyes he saw the fiery tongues lick up his treasures.

Even the Gift-seat of the Goths melted in fire.

Then was the good king sorrowful. His heart boiled within him with angry thoughts. The Fire-Dragon had utterly destroyed the pleasant homes of his people. For this the war-prince greatly desired to punish him.

Therefore did Beowulf command that a great shield should be made for him, all of iron. He knew well that a shield of wood could not help him in this need. Wood against fire! Nay, that were useless. His shield must be all of iron.

Too proud, too, was Beowulf, the hero of old time, to seek the winged beast with a troop of soldiers. Not thus would he overcome him. He feared not for himself, nor did he dread the Dragon's war-craft. For with his valour and his skill Beowulf had succeeded many a time. He had been victorious in many a tumult of battle since that day when a young man and a warrior prosperous in victory, he had cleansed Hart Hall by grappling with Grendel and his kin.

And now when the great iron shield was ready, he chose eleven of his best thanes and set out to seek the Dragon. Very wrathful was the old king, very desirous that death should take his fiery foe. He hoped, too, to win the great treasure of gold which the fell beast guarded. For already Beowulf had learned whence the feud arose, whence came the anger which had been so hurtful to his people. And the precious cup, the cause of all the quarrel, had been brought to him.

With the band of warriors went the slave who had stolen the cup. He it was who must be their guide to the cave, for he alone of all men living knew the way thither. Loth he was to be their guide. But captive and bound he was forced to lead the way over the plain to the Dragon's hill.

Unwillingly he went with lagging footsteps until at length he came to the cave hard by the sea-shore. There by the sounding waves lay the savage guardian of the treasure. Ready for war and fierce was he. It was no easy battle that was there prepared for any man, brave though he might be.

And now on the rocky point above the sea King Beowulf sat himself down. Here he would bid farewell to all his thanes ere he began the combat. For what man might tell which from that fight should come forth victorious?

Beowulf's mind was sad. He was now old. His hair was white, his face was wrinkled and grey. But still his arm was strong as that of a young man. Yet something within him warned him that death was not far off.

So upon the rocky point he sat and bade farewell to his dear comrades.

'In my youth,' said the aged king, 'many battles have I dared, and yet must I, the guardian of my people, though I be full of years, seek still another feud. And again will I win glory if the wicked spoiler of my land will but come forth from his lair.'

Much he spoke. With loving words he bade farewell to each one of his men, greeting his dear comrades for the last time.

'I would not bear a sword or weapon against the winged beast,' he said at length, 'if I knew how else I might grapple with the wretch, as of old I did with Grendel. But I ween this war-fire is hot, fierce, and poisonous. Therefore I have clad me in a coat of mail, and bear this shield all of iron. I will not flee a single step from the guardian of the treasure. But to us upon this rampart it shall be as fate will.

'Now let me make no more vaunting speech. Ready to fight am I. Let me forth against the winged beast. Await ye here on the mount, clad in your coats of mail, your arms ready. Abide ye here until ye see which of us twain in safety cometh forth from the clash of battle.

'It is no enterprise for you, or for any common man. It is mine alone. Alone I needs must go against the wretch and prove myself a warrior. I must with courage win the gold, or else deadly, baleful war shall fiercely snatch me, your lord, from life.'

Then Beowulf arose. He was all clad in shining armour, his gold-decked helmet was upon his head, and taking his shield in hand he strode under the stony cliffs towards the cavern's mouth. In the strength of his single arm he trusted against the fiery Dragon.

No enterprise this for a coward.

Chapter IX. How Beowulf Overcame the Dragon

Beowulf left his comrades upon the rocky point jutting out into the sea, and alone he strode onward until he spied a great stone arch. From beneath the arch, from out the hillside, flowed a stream seething with fierce, hot fire. In this way the Dragon guarded his lair, for it was impossible to pass such a barrier unhurt.

So upon the edge of this burning river Beowulf stood and called aloud in anger. Stout of heart and wroth against the winged beast was he.

The king's voice echoed like a warcry through the cavern. The Dragon heard it and was aroused to fresh hate of man. For the guardian of the treasure-hoard knew well the sound of mortal voice. Now was there no long pause ere battle raged.

First from out the cavern flamed forth the breath of the winged beast. Hot sweat of battle rose from out the rock. The earth shook and growling thunder trembled through the air.

The Dragon, ringed around with many-coloured scales, was now hot for battle, and, as the hideous beast crept forth, Beowulf raised his mighty shield and rushed against him.

Already the king had drawn his sword. It was an ancient heirloom, keen of edge and bright. Many a time it had been dyed in blood; many a time it had won glory and victory.

But ere they closed, the mighty foes paused. Each knew the hate and deadly power of the other.

The mighty prince, firm and watchful, stood guarded by his shield. The Dragon, crouching as in ambush, awaited him.

Then suddenly like a flaming arch the Dragon bent and towered, and dashed upon the Lord of the Goths. Up swung the arm of the hero, and dealt a mighty blow to the grisly, many-coloured beast. But the famous sword was all too weak against such a foe. The edge turned and bit less strongly than its great king had need, for he was sore pressed. His shield, too, proved no strong shelter from the wrothy Dragon.

Now he belched forth flaming fire

The warlike blow made greater still the anger of the fiery foe. Now he belched forth flaming fire. All around fierce lightnings darted.

Beowulf no longer hoped for glorious victory. His sword had failed him. The edge was turned and blunted upon the scaly foe. He had never thought the famous steel would so ill serve him. Yet he fought on ready to lose his life in such good contest.

Again the battle paused, again the king and Dragon closed in fight. The Dragon guardian of the treasure had renewed his courage. His heart heaved and boiled with fire, and fresh strength breathed from him. Beowulf was wrapped in flame. Dire was his need.

Yet of all his comrades none came near to help. Nay, as they watched the conflict they were filled with base fear, and fled to the wood hard by for refuge.

Only one among them sorrowed for his master, and as he watched his heart was wrung with grief.

Wiglaf was this knight called, and he was Beowulf's kinsman. Now when he saw his liege lord hard pressed in battle he remembered all the favours Beowulf had heaped upon him. He remembered all the honours and the wealth which he owed to his king. Then could he no longer be still. Shield and spear he seized, but ere he sped to aid his king he turned to his comrades.

'When our lord and king gave us swords and armour,' he cried, 'did we not promise to follow him in battle whenever he had need? When he of his own will chose us for this expedition he reminded us of our fame. He said he knew us to be good warriors, bold helmet-wearers. And although indeed our liege lord thought to do this work of valour alone, without us, because more than any man he hath done glorious and rash deeds, lo! now is the day come that hath need of strength and of good warriors. Come, let us go to him. Let us help our chieftain although the grim terror of fire be hot.

'Heaven knoweth I would rather the flame would blast my body than his who gave me gold. It seemeth not fitting to me that we should bear back our shields to our homes unless we may first fell the foe and defend the life of our king. Nay, it is not of the old custom of the Goths that the king alone should suffer, that he alone should sink in battle. Our lord should be repaid for his gifts to us, and so he shall be by me even if death take us twain.'

But none would hearken to Wiglaf. So alone he sped through the deadly smoke and flame, till to his master's side he came offering aid.

'My lord Beowulf,' he cried, 'fight on as thou didst in thy youth-time. Erstwhile didst thou say that thou wouldest not let thy greatness sink so long as life lasteth. Defend thou thy life with all might. I will support thee to the utmost.'

When the Dragon heard these words his fury was doubled. The fell wicked beast came on again belching forth fire, such was his hatred of

men. The flame waves caught Wiglaf's shield, for it was but of wood.
It was burned utterly, so that only the boss of steel remained. His coat
of mail alone was not enough to guard the young warrior from the fiery
enemy. But right valiantly he went on fighting beneath the shelter of
Beowulf's shield now that his own was consumed to ashes by the
flames.

Then again the warlike king called to mind his ancient glories,
again he struck with main strength with his good sword upon the
monstrous head. Hate sped the blow.

But alas! as it descended the famous sword Nægling snapped
asunder. Beowulf's sword had failed him in the conflict, although it
was an old and well-wrought blade. To him it was not granted that
weapons should help him in battle. The hand that swung the sword was
too strong. His might overtaxed every blade however wondrously the
smith had welded it.

And now a third time the fell Fire-Dragon was roused to wrath. He
rushed upon the king. Hot, and fiercely grim the great beast seized
Beowulf's neck in his horrid teeth. The hero's life-blood gushed forth,
the crimson stream darkly dyed his bright armour.

Then in the great king's need his warrior showed skill and courage.
Heeding not the flames from the awful mouth, Wiglaf struck the
Dragon below the neck. His hand was burned with the fire, but his
sword dived deep into the monster's body and from that moment the
flames began to abate.

The horrid teeth relaxed their hold, and Beowulf, quickly
recovering himself, drew his deadly knife. Battle-sharp and keen it was,
and with it the hero gashed the Dragon right in the middle.

The foe was conquered. Glowing in death he fell. They twain had
destroyed the winged beast. Such should a warrior be, such a thane in
need.

To the king it was a victorious moment. It was the crown of all his
deeds.

Then began the wound which the Fire-Dragon had wrought him to
burn and to swell. Beowulf soon found that baleful poison boiled in his
heart. Well knew he that the end was nigh. Lost in deep thought he sat
upon the mound and gazed wondering at the cave. Pillared and arched
with stone-work it was within, wrought by giants and dwarfs of old
time.

And to him came Wiglaf his dear warrior and tenderly bathed his
wound with water.

Then spake Beowulf, in spite of his deadly wound he spake, and all
his words were of the ending of his life, for he knew that his days of joy
upon this earth were past.

'Had a son been granted to me, to him I should have left my war-
garments. Fifty years have I ruled this people, and there has been no

king of all the nations round who durst meet me in battle. I have known joys and sorrows, but no man have I betrayed, nor many false oaths have I sworn. For all this may I rejoice, though I be now sick with mortal wounds. The Ruler of Men may not upbraid me with treachery or murder of kinsmen when my soul shall depart from its body.

He knew that his days of joy upon this earth were past

'But now, dear Wiglaf, go thou quickly to the hoard of gold which lieth under the hoary rock. The Dragon lieth dead; now sleepeth he for ever, sorely wounded and bereft of his treasure. Then haste thee, Wiglaf, for I would see the ancient wealth, the gold treasure, the jewels, the curious gems. Haste thee to bring it hither; then after that I have seen it, I shall the more contentedly give up my life and the kingship that I so long have held.'

Quickly Wiglaf obeyed his wounded lord. Into the dark cave he descended, and there outspread before him was a wondrous sight. Treasure of jewels, many glittering and golden, lay upon the ground. Wondrous vessels of old time with broken ornaments were scattered round. Here, too, lay old and rusty helmets, mingled with bracelets and collars cunningly wrought.

Upon the walls too hung golden flags. From one a light shone forth by which the whole cavern was made clear. And all within was silent. No sign was there of any guardian, for without lay the Dragon, sleeping death's sleep.

Quickly Wiglaf gathered of the treasures all that he could carry. Dishes and cups he took, a golden ensign and a sword curiously wrought. In haste he returned, for he knew not if still he should find his lord in life where he had left him.

And when Wiglaf came again to where Beowulf sat he poured the treasure at his feet. But he found his lord in a deep swoon. Again the brave warrior bathed Beowulf's wound and laved the stricken countenance of his lord, until once more he came to himself.

Then spake the king: 'For this treasure I give thanks to the Lord of All. Not in vain have I given my life, for it shall be of great good to my people in need. And now leave me, for on this earth longer I may not stay. Say to my warriors that they shall raise a mound upon the rocky point which jutteth seaward. High shall it stand as a memorial to my people. Let it soar upward so that they who steer their slender barks over the tossing waves shall call it Beowulf's mound.'

The king then took from his neck the golden collar. To Wiglaf, his young thane and kinsman, he gave it. He gave also his helmet adorned with gold, his ring and coat of mail, and bade the warrior use them well.

'Thou art the last of our race,' he said. 'Fate hath swept away all my kinsmen, all the mighty earls. Now must I too follow them.'

That was the last word of the aged king. From his bosom the soul fled to seek the dwellings of the Just. At Wiglaf's feet he lay quiet and still.

Chapter X. Beowulf's Last Rest

Then was the heart of Wiglaf sad when he saw upon the earth his dearest king lie still. His slayer, the frightful Fire-Dragon, lay there too. No more would he fly through the midnight air working deadly harm, no more would he guard his treasure. Beowulf had conquered him, but his victory was repaid in death.

Sorrowing, Wiglaf knelt beside his lord. He bathed his face with water, he called to him to awake. But it was of no avail. He could not, however much he longed, call back his king to earth. No prayers could turn back the doom which God the ruler had sent forth.

Now that the fight was over, it was not long before the cowards, who during all the combat had forsaken their king and sheltered in the wood, came forth. Dastard faith breakers, ten of them together now came to the place where Wiglaf knelt beside his king. They durst not draw the sword to aid at this their liege lord's need. But now ashamed, they came bearing their shields, wearing their war-garments now that all need of them was past.

Then Wiglaf, sorrowful in soul, looked with anger at the cowards. No soft words had he for the craven-hearted crew.

'Lo,' he cried, 'he that would speak truth may well say that the liege lord who gave you these war-garments in which ye stand utterly castaway his gifts. Helmets and coats of mail he gave to those he deemed most worthy. But when war came upon him truly the king had little cause to boast of his warriors. Yet the Lord of All, the Ruler of Victories, granted him valour so that he avenged himself alone with his sword. I could give him in the combat little protection and aid. Yet I undertook above my means to help my kinsman. Weak I am, yet when I struck with my sword the Dragon's fire flamed less fiercely. When I smote the destroyer, fire gushed less violently forth from him.

'Too few defenders thronged round their prince when need came. And now for you there shall be no more sharing of treasure, no more giving of swords, no more joy in your homes. Houseless and beggared shall ye wander when far and wide the nobles shall hear of your flight, of your base deed. Death is better for every warrior than a life of shame.'

Then Wiglaf turned from the cowards in scorn. Up over the sea cliff a troop of warriors had sat all day from early morn awaiting the return of their king. To them Wiglaf commanded that the issue of the fight should now be told.

So a messenger rode to the cliff. Loud he spake so that all might hear his baleful news. 'Now is the kind Lord of the Goth folk fast on his deathbed. He resteth on his fatal couch through the Dragon's deed. By him lieth his deadly foe done to death with sword-wounds. Beside Beowulf, Wiglaf, sits. One warrior over another lifeless holdeth sorrowful ward 'gainst friend or foe.

'Now may the people of the Danes expect a time of war. For as soon as the fall of the king be known among the Franks and Frisians they will make battle-ready. Yea, such is the deadly hate of men, that I ween from all around they will attack us when they shall learn our lord is lifeless. For he it was who defended our land against the foe. He it was who kept safe both treasure and realm with his wisdom and valour.

'Now it were best that with all speed we brought the great king to the funeral pile. It is not meet that treasure of little value be buried with the bold king. For here lieth a house of treasure, of gold uncounted, sadly bought with his life's blood. These the fire must devour, the flame must enwrap. No warrior shall wear bracelet or collar for remembrance. No fair maiden shall deck her neck with the gold's sheen. Nay rather, sad of mood, with golden ornaments laid aside, often shall they tread a strange land now that our war leader has ceased from laughter, from sport, and from song of joy. No longer now shall sound of harp awaken the warriors; but the hand that held the sword shall lie cold. The dark raven over the dead shall croak, he shall tell the eagle how he sped with his meal, while the wolf spoiled the carcasses of the slain.'

Thus spake the bold warrior, bringer of evil tidings.

And now the troop all arose. Sadly and with welling tears they went under the cliff-ways to behold the fearful sight.

They found upon the sand, lifeless and soulless, him who before time had given them gifts. So was the end, and the good chief was gone. He in death heroic had perished.

There too they saw a more strange thing. Near the king lay the Dragon all loathly along the plain. Fifty feet long he lay scorched with his own fires, grim and ghastly to look upon. He who of old joyed to fly through the air in the night-time now lay fast in death. Never more would he fly through the air, never more gloat in his cave. By him stood cups and vessels, dishes and precious swords, rusty and eaten away. They seemed as if they had lain a thousand years in the earth.

Then Wiglaf lifted up his voice and spake. 'Often must a brave man endure sorrow for another, as it hath happened with us. We could in no wise hold our king back from this combat. The hoard here hath been dearly bought. I have been within and beheld all the treasures of the cave. As much as I could carry I bore out to my lord who was yet living. Then many things spake he, the wise king. He bade me greet you, prayed that ye would make a lofty cairn, great and glorious, upon the coast here, for he was a warrior most famous throughout all the earth. Come now, let us hasten a second time to see and seek the wonders within the cave. I will be your guide, and ye shall see rings and piled gold such as ye have gazed upon never before.

'Let the bier be made ready against our return. Then let us bear our lord to the place where he shall long rest in the peace of the All-Powerful.'

Then did Wiglaf send commandment to all those who possessed land, houses, and slaves, that they should bring wood for the pile for the funeral of the good king.

'Now,' he said, 'shall the flame devour, the wan fire and the flame shall grow strong, and shall destroy the prince of warriors. He who so often in the thickest of the fight awaited the storm of darts shall now depart hence for evermore.'

Then having given commandment that the people should build the funeral pile, Wiglaf called seven of the best of the king's thanes to him.

With them he went into the dark treasure-cavern.

Before them marched a warrior bearing in his hand a flaming torch. And when they saw the treasure lying around, gold and jewels in countless numbers, the thanes marvelled greatly. Quickly they gathered of the hoard and carried it forth. A great wagon they loaded with twisted gold and all manner of precious stuffs, and brought it to the funeral pile.

As for the winged beast which lay dead upon the plain, they thrust it over the cliff into the sea below. There he sank, and the waves closed over the dead guardian of the treasure of which the cave was now all despoiled.

And now the aged warrior was laid upon a bier. Then with bowed heads and lagging steps his thanes bore him to the cliff where high above the sea the funeral pile was laid.

Roundabout it was hung with helmets and with shields and with bright coats of mail. And in the midst was laid the great king, while the warriors mourned and wept for their beloved lord.

Then the funeral pyre was lit. Great flames sprang upward, dark clouds of smoke rolled up to the sky. The roar of the flame was mingled with the weeping of the Goth people, as with heavy hearts in woful mood they mourned the death of their liege lord.

Then a dirge of sorrow was sung by an aged dame in honour of Beowulf. Again and again she wailed forth her sore dread of evil days to come. Much blood-shed, shame, and captivity would come upon the land, she cried, now that its lord was dead.

And as she wailed the fire flamed and roared until the wood was all burned away. Then the great pyre sank together in ashes: the body of the great king was all consumed in flame.

Then did the Goth people build a high cairn upon the hill where the fire had been. It was high and broad, and might be seen for many miles by the travellers upon the sea. For ten days they built up the beacon of the war-renowned, famous king. They surrounded it with a wall in the most honourable manner that wise men could devise. Within the cairn they placed the rings and bright jewels and all manner of precious ornaments which they had taken from the Dragon's hoard. And thus they left the great treasure to the earth to hold. Gold they laid in the dust, where it yet remains to men as useless as of old. Then round the cairn twelve war-chiefs slowly rode. And as they rode they spoke and sang of their king.

They praised his valour, they sang of his manhood and his courtesy. Even so it is fitting that a man should praise his liege lord and love him.

Thus the Goth people wept for their fallen lord. His comrades said that he was of all the kings of the earth the best. Of men he was the mildest and the kindest, and to his people the gentlest. Of all rulers he was most worthy of praise.

Thus went the great king to his last rest.

THE END